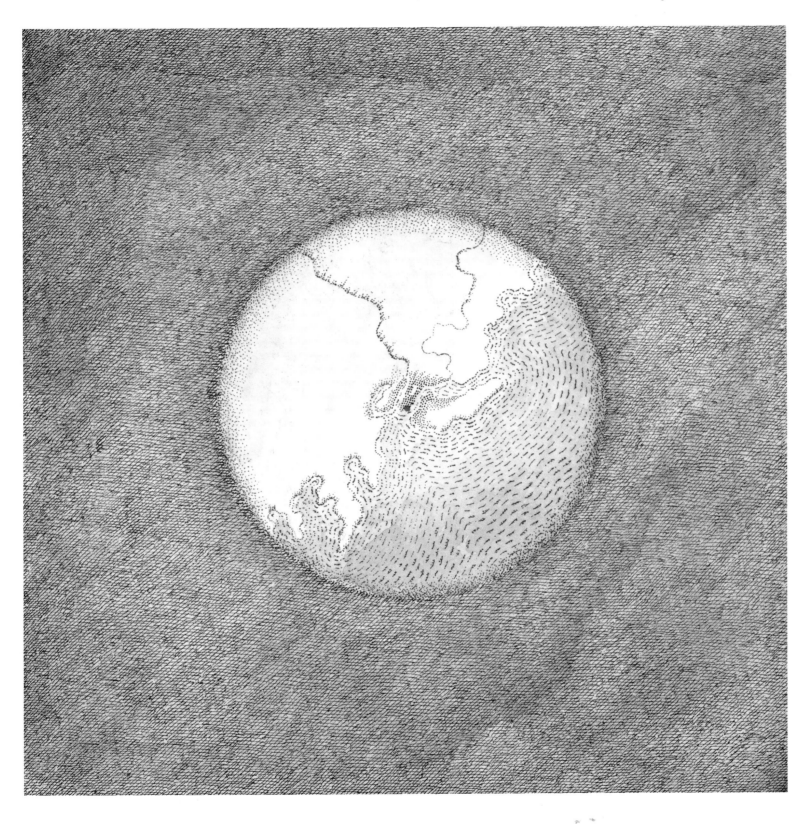

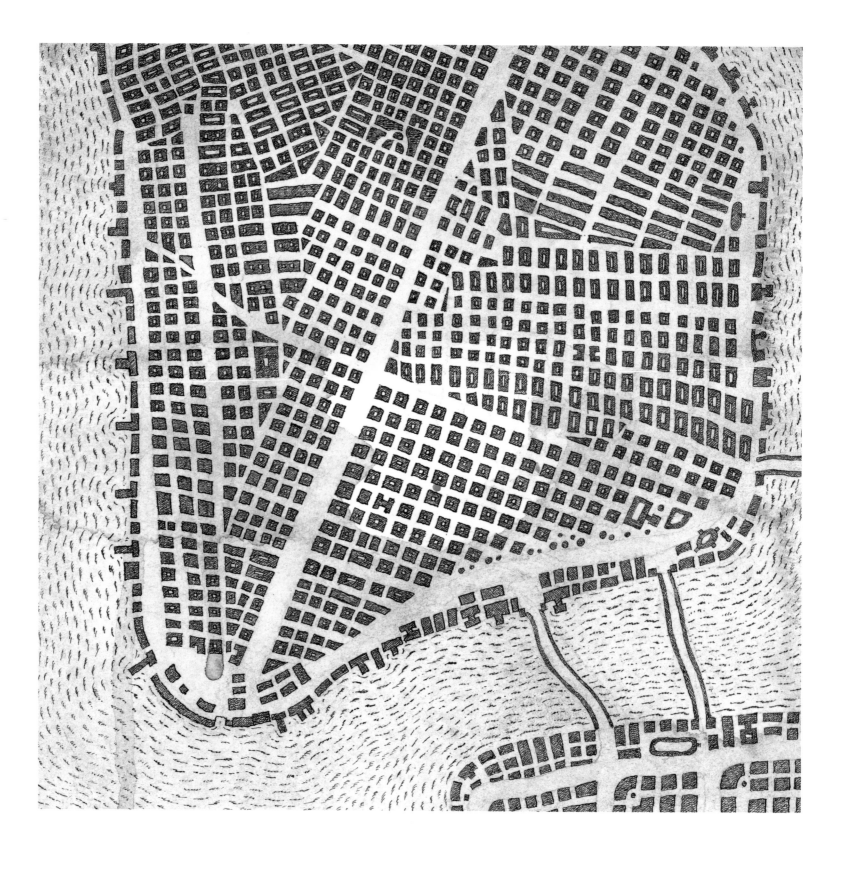

MADLENKA

Peter Sís

SCHOLASTIC INC.

New York Toronto London Auckland Sydney
Mexico City New Delhi Hong Kong

in a country, in a city, on a block, in a house,

In the universe, on a planet, on a continent,

in a window, in the rain, a little girl named

Madlenka

finds out her tooth wiggles.

She has to tell everyone.

Hey, everyone . . . my tooth is loose!

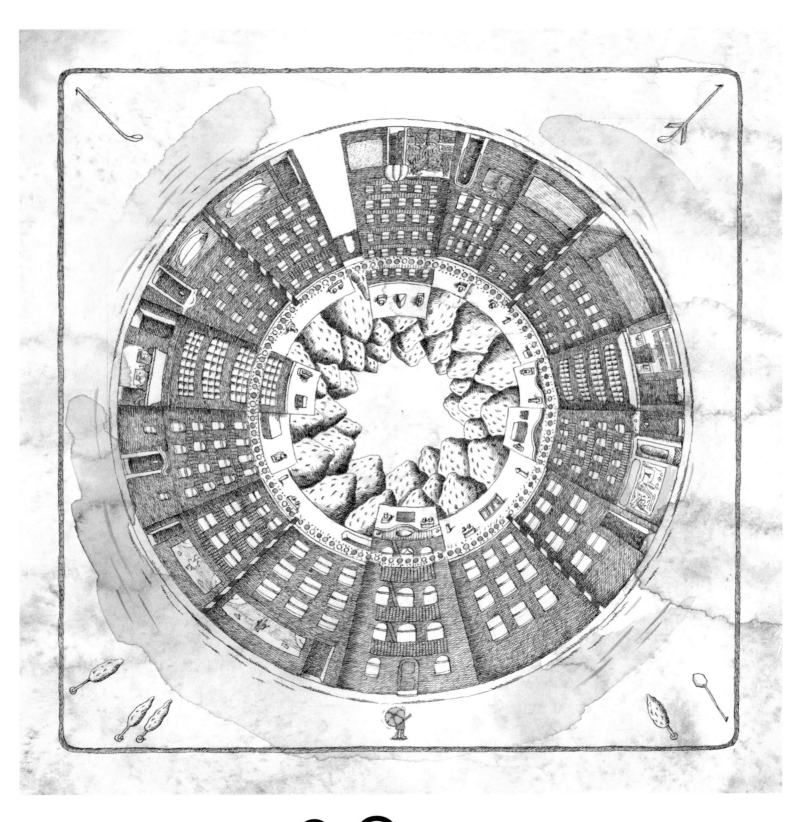

LOOOSE

Jumping with joy, she skips down the street
and sees her friend Mr. Gaston, the French baker.

CROISSANTS

MADELEINES

CHOCOLATE CAKES

FRENCH BREAD

CAKES WITH FRUIT

FINANCIERS

WHEN I HAVE
A BIRTHDAY
HE PUTS A PINK
BALLERINA
ON MY CAKE · · · →

HE TELLS ME ABOUT PARIS

AND ABOUT FRANCE

MR. GASTON BAKES

I AM
A BIG
GIRL
NOW

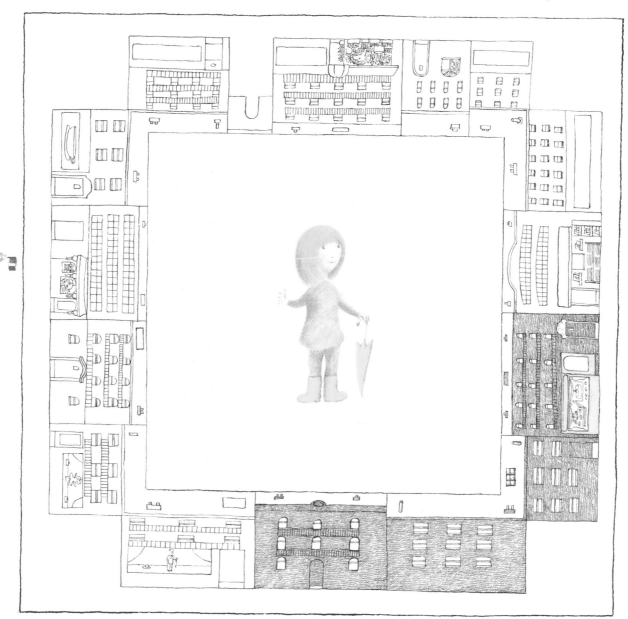

HELLO, MR. GASTON · MY TOOTH IS LOOSE!

Bonjour, Madeleine. Let's celebrate.

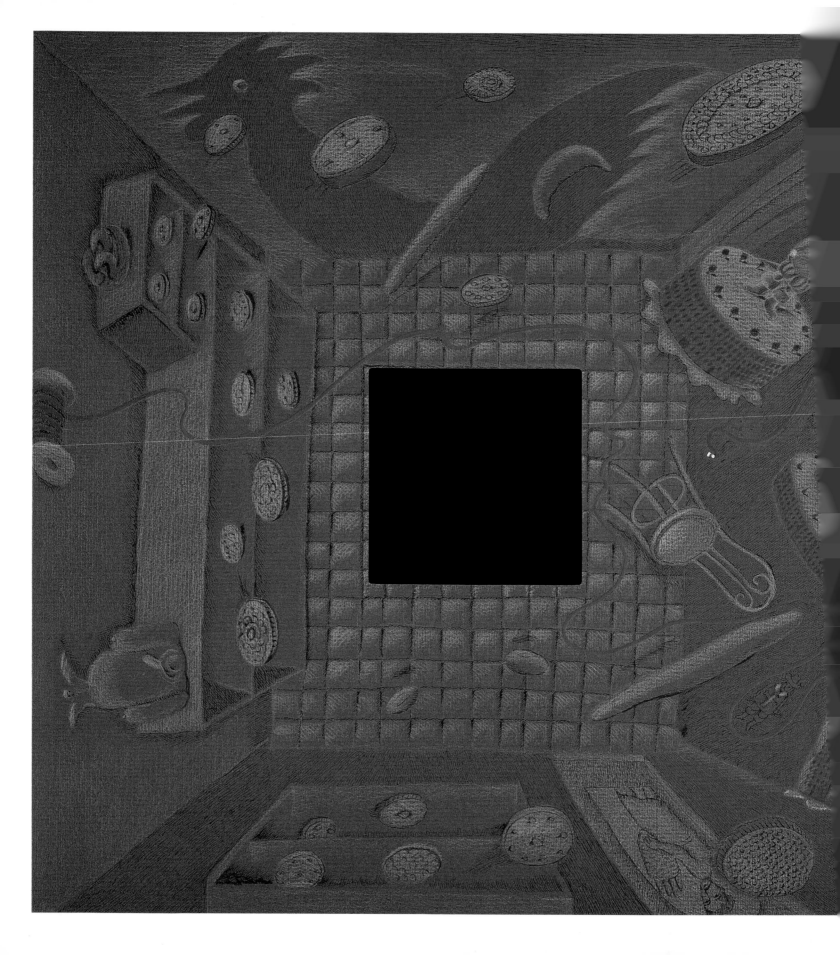

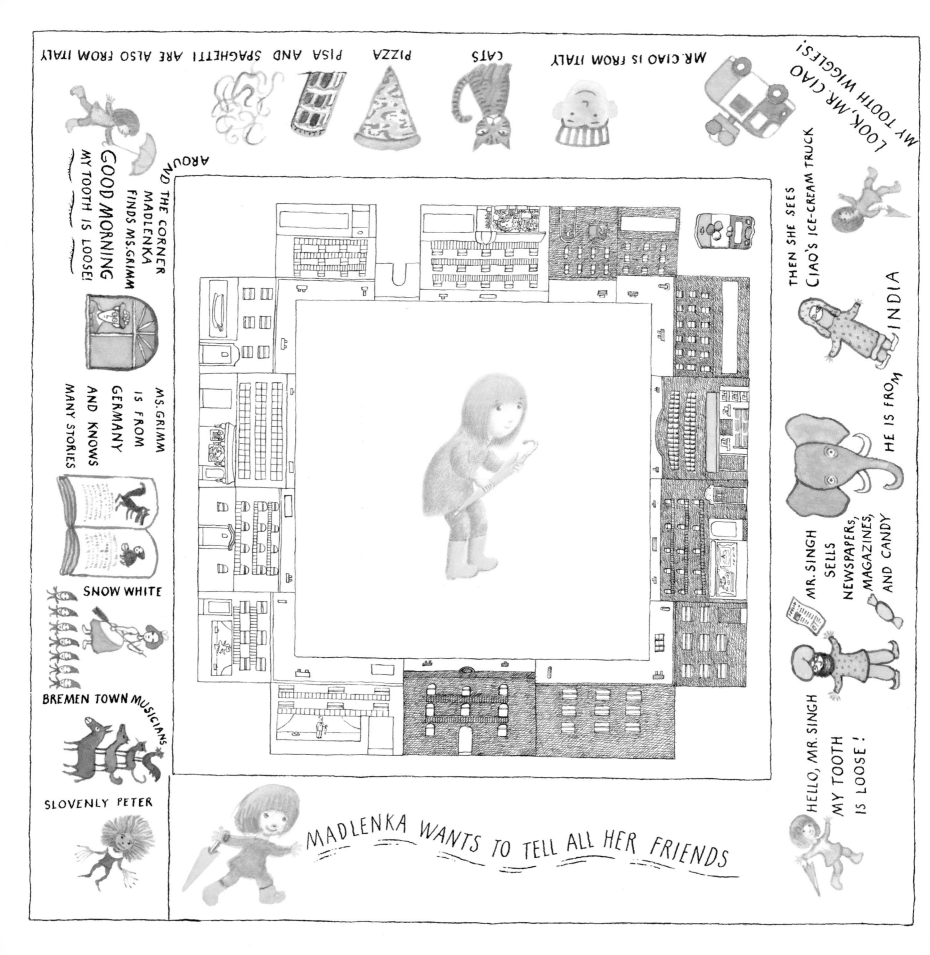

GOOD MORNING
MY TOOTH IS LOOSE!

AROUND THE CORNER MADLENKA FINDS MS.GRIMM

MS.GRIMM IS FROM GERMANY AND KNOWS MANY STORIES

SNOW WHITE

BREMEN TOWN MUSICIANS

SLOVENLY PETER

PISA AND SPAGHETTI ARE ALSO FROM ITALY

PIZZA

CATS

MR.CIAO IS FROM ITALY

LOOK, MR.CIAO
MY TOOTH WIGGLES!

THEN SHE SEES CIAO'S ICE-CREAM TRUCK

HE IS FROM INDIA

MR.SINGH SELLS NEWSPAPERS, MAGAZINES, AND CANDY

HELLO, MR. SINGH
MY TOOTH IS LOOSE!

MADLENKA WANTS TO TELL ALL HER FRIENDS

Sathsariakal, Madela. Good news!

Buon giorno, Maddalena.
This calls for a treat.

Guten Tag, Magda. Let me tell you a story.

Madlenka thinks this must be the best day of her life.

Oh, there's Mr. Eduardo, the greengrocer.

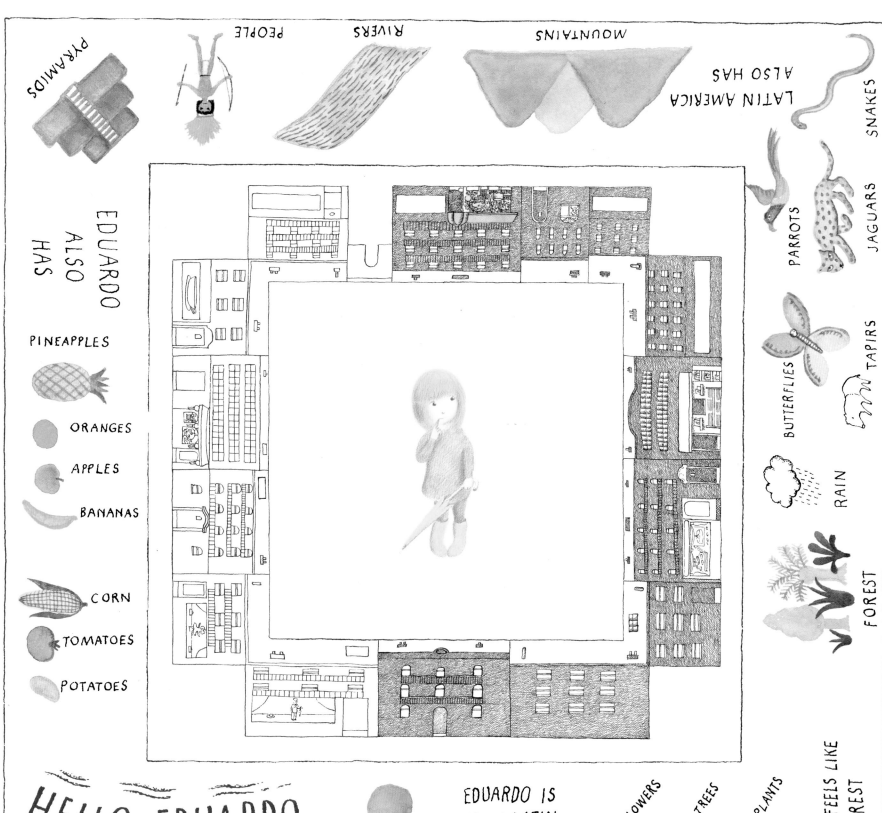

PYRAMIDS

PEOPLE

RIVERS

MOUNTAINS

LATIN AMERICA ALSO HAS

SNAKES

JAGUARS

PARROTS

BUTTERFLIES

TAPIRS

RAIN

FOREST

EDUARDO ALSO HAS

PINEAPPLES

ORANGES

APPLES

BANANAS

CORN

TOMATOES

POTATOES

HELLO, EDUARDO

MY TOOTH WIGGLES!

EDUARDO IS FROM LATIN AMERICA

HE SELLS

FLOWERS

TREES

PLANTS

HIS STORE FEELS LIKE A RAIN FOREST

Hola, Magdalena. Señorita Magdalena!

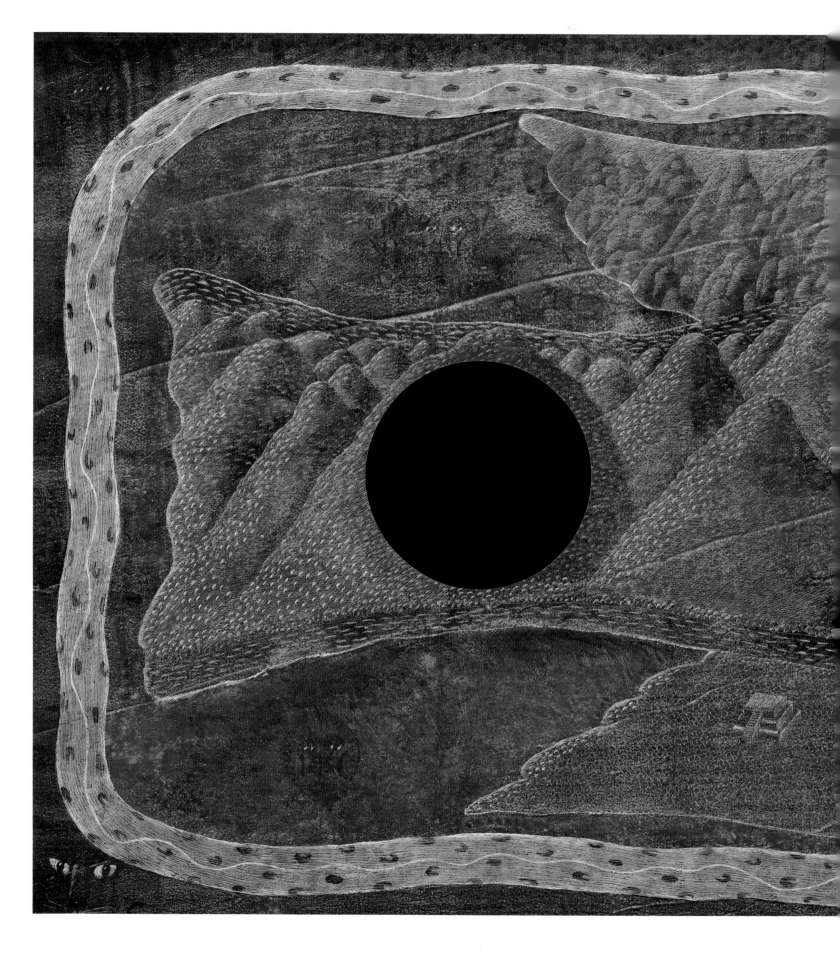

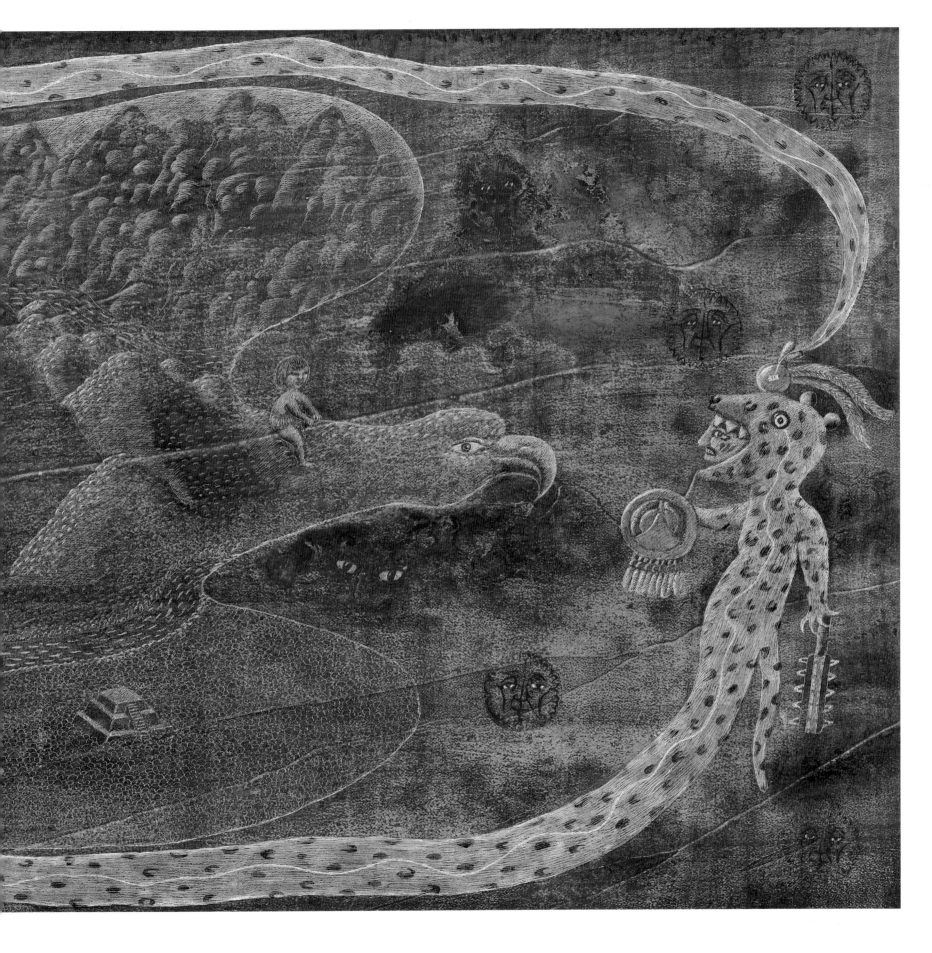

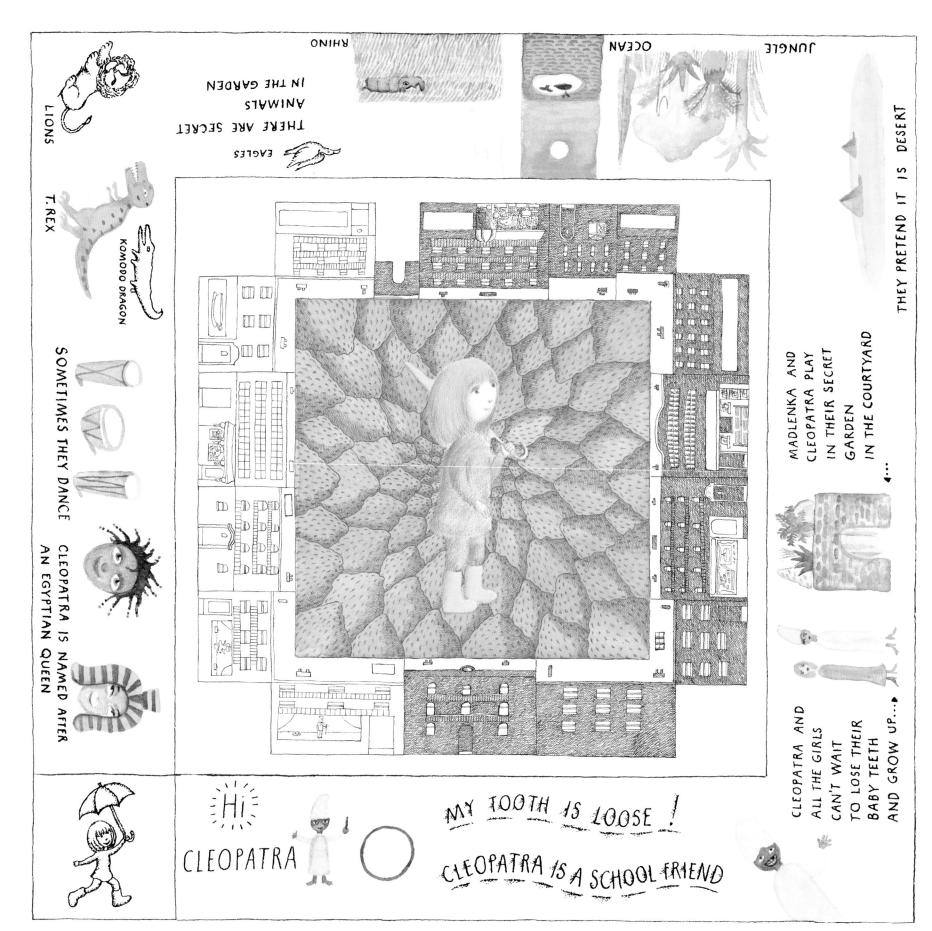

LIONS

T.REX

KOMODO DRAGON

SOMETIMES THEY DANCE

CLEOPATRA IS NAMED AFTER
AN EGYPTIAN QUEEN

EAGLES

THERE ARE SECRET
ANIMALS
IN THE GARDEN

RHINO

OCEAN

JUNGLE

THEY PRETEND IT IS DESERT

MADLENKA AND
CLEOPATRA PLAY
IN THEIR SECRET
GARDEN
IN THE COURTYARD

CLEOPATRA AND
ALL THE GIRLS
CAN'T WAIT
TO LOSE THEIR
BABY TEETH
AND GROW UP...

HI

CLEOPATRA

MY TOOTH IS LOOSE !

CLEOPATRA IS A SCHOOL FRIEND

Cool, baby. Let's play in the courtyard.

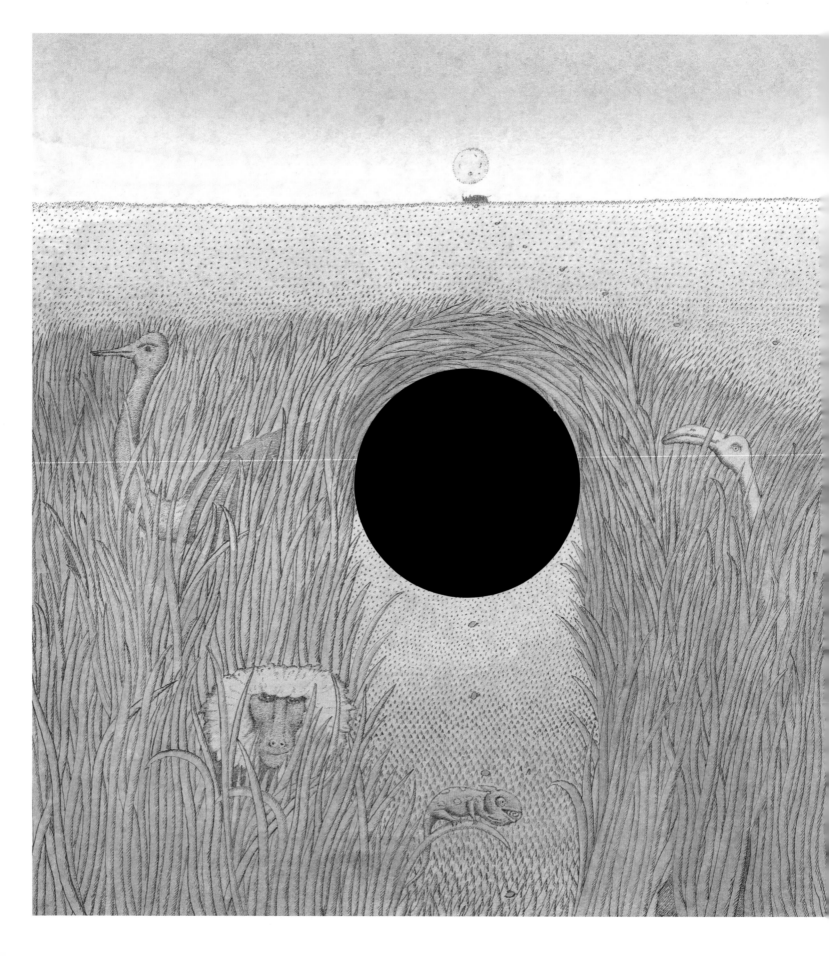

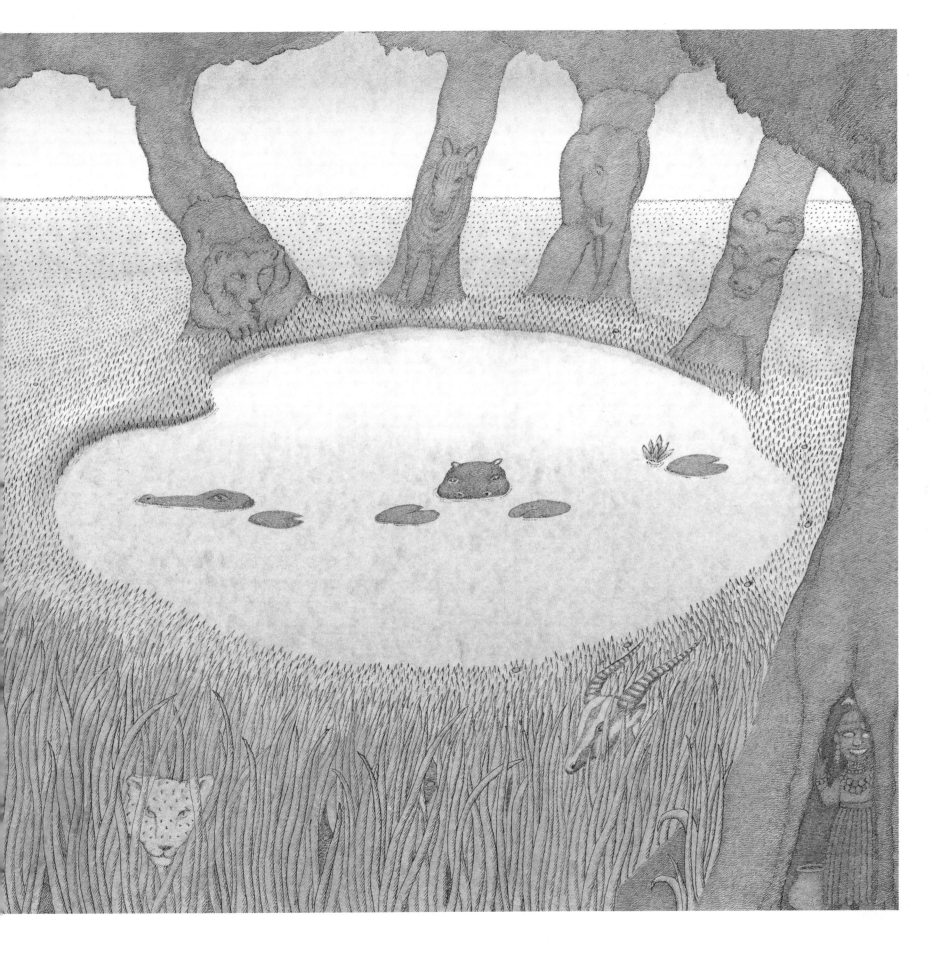

Who else can she tell?

Oh! Mrs. Kham has to know.

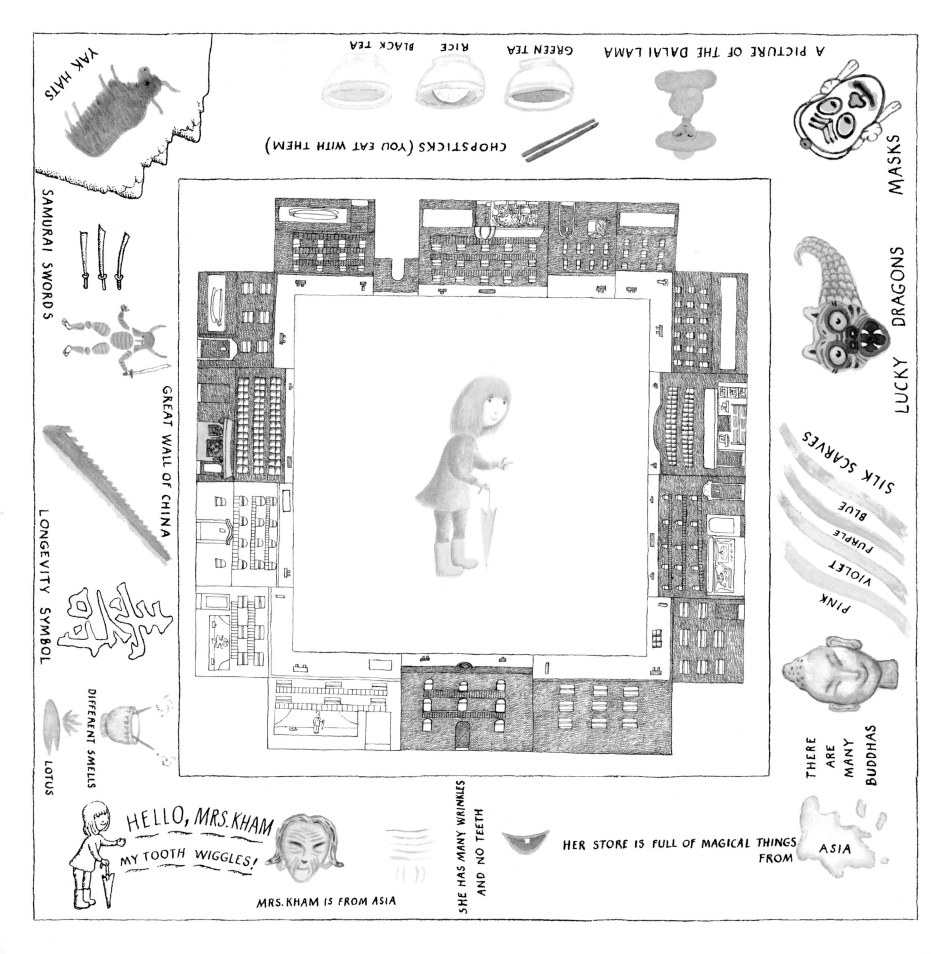

YAK HATS

BLACK TEA

RICE

GREEN TEA

A PICTURE OF THE DALAI LAMA

CHOPSTICKS (YOU EAT WITH THEM)

MASKS

SAMURAI SWORDS

LUCKY DRAGONS

GREAT WALL OF CHINA

SILK SCARVES

BLUE

PURPLE

VIOLET

PINK

LONGEVITY SYMBOL

DIFFERENT SMELLS

LOTUS

THERE ARE MANY BUDDHAS

HELLO, MRS. KHAM

MY TOOTH WIGGLES!

SHE HAS MANY WRINKLES AND NO TEETH

HER STORE IS FULL OF MAGICAL THINGS FROM ASIA

MRS. KHAM IS FROM ASIA

Tashi delek, Mandala. That's a lucky sign.

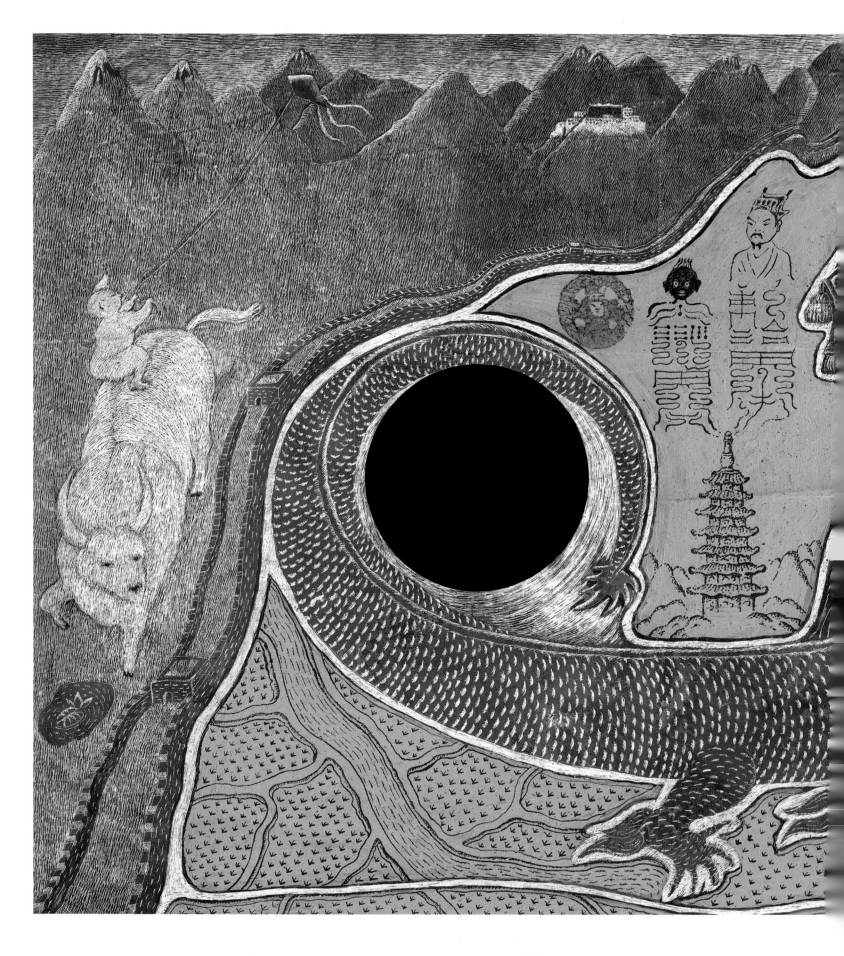

Oh dear. I'm late.

Madlenka! Where have you been?

Well . . . I went around the world.

And I lost my tooth!

TO TERRY-MADELEINE-MATEJ-ALL BORN IN NEW YORK CITY

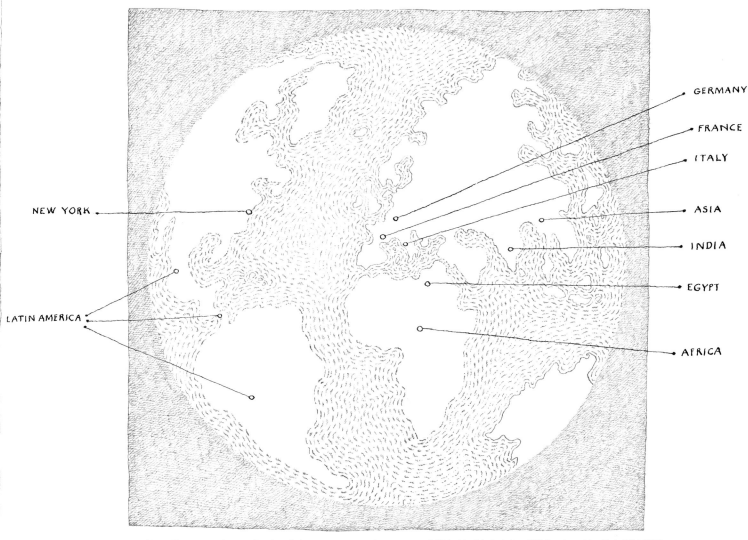

NEW YORK

LATIN AMERICA

GERMANY

FRANCE

ITALY

ASIA

INDIA

EGYPT

AFRICA

ISBN 0-439-23313-5

Published by Scholastic Inc., 555 Broadway, New York, NY 10012, by arrangement with Farrar, Straus and Giroux, Inc. SCHOLASTIC and associated logos are trademarks and/or registered trademarks of Scholastic Inc.

12 11 10 9 8 7 6 5 4 3 2 1   0 1 2 3 4 5/0

Printed in Hong Kong

First Scholastic printing, October 2000 Typography by Filomena Tuosto.

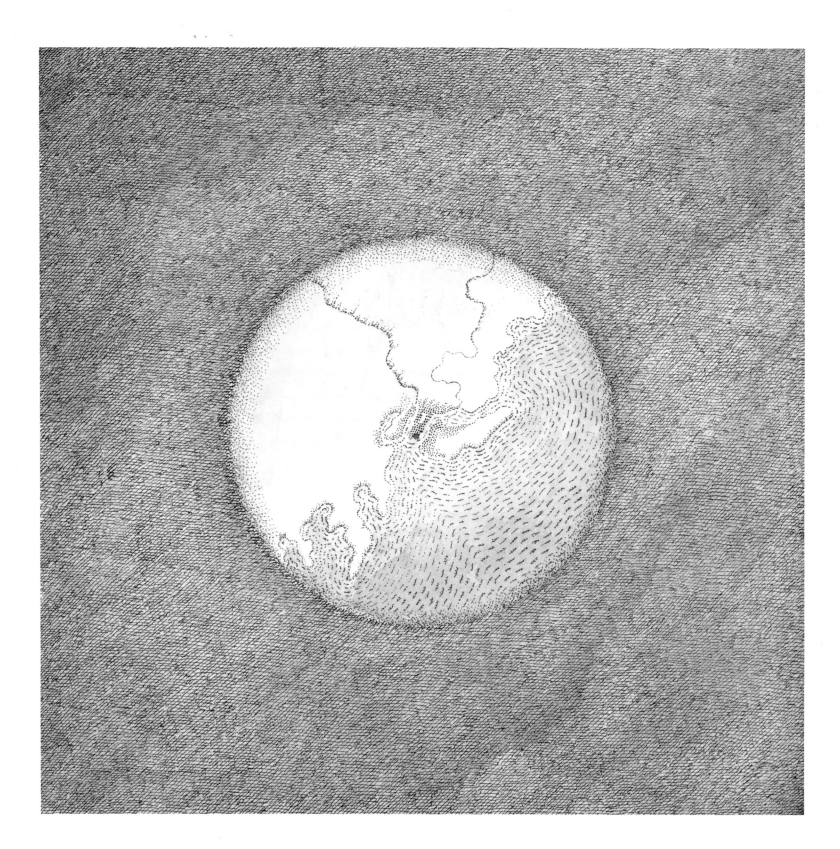